SATURDAY AT THE FOOD PANTRY

Diane O'Neill

illustrated by Brizida Magro

Albert Whitman & Company
Chicago, Illinois

To Tyrone, my son and my friend. Thanks for all the moral support you've given your writer mom!—DO

To Avó (Grandmother), for keeping me safe, warm, and full—BM

Library of Congress Cataloging-in-Publication data
is on file with the publisher.
Text copyright © 2021 by Diane O'Neill
Illustrations copyright © 2021 by Albert Whitman & Company
Illustrations by Brizida Magro
First published in the United States of America
in 2021 by Albert Whitman & Company
ISBN 978-0-8075-7236-8 (hardcover)
ISBN 978-0-8075-7238-2 (ebook)

Printed in the United States of America
10 9 8 7 6 5 4 3 2 JOS 26 25 24 23 22 21

Design by Valerie Hernández

For more information about Albert Whitman & Company,
visit our website at www.albertwhitman.com.

"Dinner!" Mom called.

"Chili again?" Molly asked.

They'd had it every day this week. Last week too.

"Yup," Mom said. "Tastes even better—the spices sink in."

Mom ladled the last of the chili into their bowls.

"We have fancy milk too."

Molly grinned. She watched Mom pour milk into the sugar and spices in her cup.

Mom shook the milk carton—just a tiny splash—and put it in the refrigerator.

"Tomorrow, we'll get food," Mom said.

"We're going shopping?" Molly's eyes lit up. Chicken and spaghetti and ice cream!

"Well, sort of. We're going to a food pantry."

"What's a food pantry?" Molly asked.

"It's a place for people who need food." Mom stood straight, her chin high.

"Everybody needs help sometimes."

At bedtime, Mom usually made warm fancy milk and read a story.

Tonight, just a story.

Molly tossed and turned, trying to sleep. Her hunger growled.

The next morning, they walked to the food pantry.

"Why do we need to wait?" Molly asked.

"The pantry isn't open yet," Mom said. "It's only open certain hours."

Molly pulled paper and crayons out of
her backpack. She started drawing.

Then she looked up.

"Look, Mom, there's Caitlin. She's in my class. Hey, Caitlin!"

Caitlin looked away.

Molly ran over to her. "Didn't you hear me?"

Caitlin looked down. "I don't want anybody to know Gran
and I need help," she whispered.
"Oh." Molly walked back to her mom.

Was there something wrong with needing help?

Molly wanted to go home. But she was hungry.

"You okay?" Mom asked. "Why don't you draw me a picture? I love your drawings."

The woman in front of them turned, smiling at Molly. "An artist! Will you draw one for me too?"

Molly pulled out her crayons again. Maybe drawing a happy picture would cheer her up.

"Hey, can you draw me a picture too?"

"Me too!"

"Will you draw me one?"

Molly ran to Caitlin with paper and crayons
in her hands. "Help! Everybody wants pictures.
I can't draw that fast!"

Caitlin looked up. "Well—okay."

WELCOME TO THE
FOOD PANTRY

Soon, a woman opened the door. Molly and
Caitlin each handed her a picture.

"Thank you! What wonderful gifts."

"Welcome! Please sign in," said the man at the desk.

Mom didn't have to sign her name when they went to the grocery store, Molly thought.

But the man smiled at them. "Thanks! Grab a cart, and stop here when you're done. Lots of good food today."

"Thanks," Mom said. She smiled, but just a little, not like when they played in the park.

The food pantry was like the little store where they sometimes bought bread and milk. Cans and boxes were on plain metal shelves.

Molly ran toward a shelf and picked up a box of sugar cookies.

"No!" Mom said. Then she whispered. "They—the people in charge— they'll want us to take sensible stuff." Mom's face turned pink.

Molly's eyes widened. Why did her mom think that? Why were cookies here, if you weren't supposed to take them?

The woman at the door and the man at the desk had seemed nice. Would they really not want Molly and her mom to have cookies?

Molly swallowed tears. She put the cookies back. They would've been good with fancy milk.

"Help me put food in the cart." Mom sighed.

Just like Caitlin, Mom looked like she wanted to be invisible.

But none of them were doing anything wrong!

"Everybody needs help sometimes," Molly whispered to her mom. "Remember?"

Mom smiled. "You're right."

Molly pointed at a sign on a huge bin of fruit. "What if somebody wants two cantaloupes?"

"A lot of people need help," Mom said. "They have to make sure they have enough food for everybody who comes here."

Molly and Mom put oranges and a cantaloupe in their cart.

ONLY

PEACHES PEACHES
PEACHES PEACHES
PEACHES PEACHES

PASTA

TOMATOES

TOMATOES

PINTO BEANS PINTO BEANS
PINTO BEANS PINTO BEANS

TAKE ONE ONL

Mom handed Molly cans of corn, tomatoes, and cling peaches.

Bags of red beans, pinto beans, and brown rice.

A loaf of wheat bread, a box of oatmeal, and a bag of sugar.

Spaghetti noodles, sauce, and grated cheese.

Raisins and tuna and peanut butter too.

Mom reached for a big box of powdered milk.

"We'll have fancy milk tonight."

They checked out at the desk. The man pointed to the wall.

"Ooh!" Molly ran to Caitlin. "Come here! Look!"

Molly's rainbow sparkled. Caitlin's elf grinned.

"I was in a sad mood," the man said. "Your artwork helped—thank you!"

He put their groceries into bags. Then he handed Molly's mom a box of sugar cookies. "Saw your little girl looking at these. She can have them, if that's okay with you, ma'am."

Mom had a funny look, almost like she wanted to cry. She nodded. "Thank you."

"Everybody deserves a treat," the man said. "Enjoy!"

Molly and Mom walked home. They each carried a bulging bag.

"Molly!"

She looked around and saw Caitlin and her gran.

"I didn't know you lived so close," Mom said to Caitlin's gran.

"How nice—we're neighbors," Caitlin's gran said.

"I keep looking for work—they closed the factory," Mom said.

"I've been sick," said Caitlin's gran.

"We got lots of yummy food," Molly said. "Did you?"

"Yeah." Caitlin shrugged. "I just wish we didn't have to come to a food pantry."

Molly said, "But everybody needs help sometimes.
And we helped. We cheered people up."

Caitlin grinned. "We did, didn't we?"

"I have an idea—let's have lunch together," Molly said.

"Yes!" Caitlin agreed.

"And we have dessert," Molly said. "The man at the pantry gave me sugar cookies! There's enough for all of us. Let's eat!"

And they did.

A Note for Adults and Caregivers about Food Insecurity

Molly and her mother are right: everybody needs help sometimes.

There should be no shame in turning to a food pantry during a time of need. Children need nutritious food to grow, learn, and thrive.

In the United States in 2019, more than thirty-five million people struggled to consistently afford nutritious food—a socioeconomic condition often referred to as food insecurity, according to Feeding America, the nation's leading anti-hunger organization.

In 2020, that number is estimated to have increased to more than fifty million because of the coronavirus pandemic. Child hunger has also soared during this period. About one in three households with children reported having difficulty affording food, according to a 2020 study from economists at Northwestern University.

Food insecurity exists in every community, regardless of geography. People living in rural communities often face hunger at higher rates because of scarce job opportunities and longer distances to grocery stores and other sources of food.

Here in Chicago, and in other urban areas across the country, Black and Latinx communities are disproportionately affected by food insecurity because of years of racial disparities. Sadly, many communities of color have inequitable access to food, jobs, housing, and healthcare.

Food is a human right. No one should have to go hungry. Everyone should have access to fresh fruits and vegetables, protein, dairy, whole grains—and yes, Molly, the occasional cookie.

If you find yourself struggling to afford food, please contact your local food bank to find the nearest food distribution site. If you're unsure how to do that, visit www.feedingamerica.org to find the food bank serving your community. Government assistance called the Supplemental Nutrition Assistance Program (SNAP) also provides important food assistance to millions of Americans.

Food insecurity is not a permanent condition. Life can be hard and sometimes unfair, but it can get better too. Many people who turn to food pantries or SNAP often find themselves helping others in need later in life.

Together, we can help one another go from hungry to hopeful.

Kate Maehr
Executive Director & CEO
Greater Chicago Food Depository